5|14

Kelsey Green, Reading Queen

Franklin School Friends

Kelsey Green, Reading Queen

Claudia Mills

pictures by Rob Shepperson

Margaret Ferguson Books

Farrar Straus Giroux • New York

Farrar Straus Giroux Books for Young Readers
175 Fifth Avenue, New York 10010

Text copyright © 2013 by Claudia Mills
Pictures copyright © 2013 by Rob Shepperson
Printed in the United States of America
by RR Donnelley & Sons Company, Harrisonburg, Virginia
First edition, 2013
1   3   5   7   9   10   8   6   4   2

mackids.com

Library of Congress Cataloging-in-Publication Data
Mills, Claudia.
    Kelsey Green, reading queen / Claudia Mills ; pictures by Rob
Shepperson. — 1st ed.
        p.   cm.
    "Margaret Ferguson Books."
    Summary: Kelsey is the best reader in her third grade class, and
she is determined to lead her class to victory in the all-school
reading contest.
    ISBN 978-0-374-37485-3 (hardcover)
    ISBN 978-0-374-37488-4 (e-book)
    [1. Books and reading—Fiction.   2. Schools—Fiction.
3. Contests—Fiction.]   I. Shepperson, Rob, ill.   II. Title.

PZ7.M63963Ke 2012
[Fic]—dc23
                                                                2011027870

To all book lovers everywhere
—C.M.

For Jessina
—R.S.

Kelsey Green, Reading Queen

1

Kelsey Green no longer heard any of the voices in her third-grade classroom. All her attention was focused on the book spread open beneath her desk.

Would the old key that had been buried in the earth for the last ten years open the locked door to the hidden garden?

Drawing in her breath, Kelsey waited as the key fitted into the keyhole.

The key turned.

Then with a squeak, the door opened slowly . . . slowly.

"Kelsey!"

The sound of her name startled her. The voice was cross, as if it had been calling her name without success for some time.

She looked up from *The Secret Garden*. Mrs. Molina was glaring at her from the front of the classroom.

"Kelsey, the rest of us are focusing on page 163 in our math books. The rest of us are not staring down at our laps lost in a daydream. The rest of us are doing fractions."

Kelsey felt sorry for the rest of them. But now she also felt sorry for herself. She knew Mrs. Molina was waiting for her to turn her full attention to her math book—the one book in the whole world that Kelsey did not love, or even like, but actually hated.

"Question fourteen," Mrs. Molina said. "What is one-eighth plus one-eighth?"

Kelsey had no idea. She wasn't completely sure what an eighth was.

Luckily, one of her two best friends, Annika Riz, sat right behind her. Annika whispered the answer, loud enough that Kelsey could hear, but not loud enough that Mrs. Molina could hear.

"Two-eighths," Kelsey said.

"And two-eighths reduces to?"

Annika whispered the answer again.

"One-fourth," Kelsey said.

Next to her, Kelsey's other best friend, Izzy Barr, started to giggle, but stopped herself in time. Both Kelsey and Izzy were glad to be best friends with the third-grade math queen. Izzy would rather be out running than doing math. Kelsey would rather be reading than doing math. Annika loved math the way that Izzy loved running and Kelsey loved reading.

Mrs. Molina shot Kelsey a suspicious look, but called on someone else for question fifteen.

With Mrs. Molina's attention directed elsewhere, Kelsey allowed herself to glance down at the book on her lap and finish the next few lines. Mary Lennox was finally standing inside the secret garden at Misselthwaite Manor! Kelsey didn't dare turn the page to start the next chapter.

Instead, she listened as Simon Ellis got question sixteen right; Simon was good at everything. And as Cody Harmon got question seventeen wrong; Cody was bad at everything, or at least bad at math, spelling, reading, writing, science, and social studies.

Just as someone else was trying to answer question eighteen, the classroom door opened. In came the principal, Mr. Boone. Mrs. Molina's voice turned friendlier as she welcomed him into the room. She saved her stern, math-fact-quizzing voice for her third graders. But even though her voice sounded friendlier, her face didn't look any friendlier.

Mr. Boone settled himself on Mrs. Molina's desk. Kelsey could tell from the way Mrs. Molina snatched a stack of papers out of his way that she didn't approve of principals sitting on teachers' desks. Mr. Boone was large, and he took up a lot of room. Mrs. Molina moved her coffee cup far away.

The best thing about Mr. Boone was his big, booming laugh. Kelsey had never been sent to the principal's office; she wondered if Mr. Boone laughed even when naughty kids were sent to him for talking back to teachers or fighting on the playground. He would have to be strict and scolding sometimes if he was a principal, but it was hard to imagine. Mrs. Molina should be the principal, and Mr. Boone should be a third-grade teacher, preferably Kelsey's third-grade teacher.

The second best thing about Mr. Boone was his beard—a thick, bushy Santa Claus beard, but black instead of white. A pirate beard, maybe, for a jolly, good-natured pirate.

"Good morning, third graders!" Mr. Boone shouted. He gave his big, booming laugh, even though he hadn't yet said anything funny.

"I've heard that there are a lot of excellent readers in this class," Mr. Boone said.

Kelsey sat up straighter in her seat. She quickly checked to see if everyone was looking at her, but they were all busy looking at Mr. Boone. She was definitely the best reader in the class—well, except for Simon Ellis. But even though Simon read a lot of books, long ones, too, Kelsey didn't think he loved books the way she did. Nobody could love books the way she did.

"You're going to get a chance over the next month to show me exactly *how* excellent," Mr. Boone went on.

Kelsey sat up even straighter.

"We are going to have our first-ever all-school reading contest!" Mr. Boone laughed. Kelsey knew he didn't think the reading contest was a joke; he was laughing because he thought it was a gloriously happy thing.

She did, too.

"Starting tomorrow, April first, we're going to keep track of how many books each class reads. The class that reads the most books will have a pizza party with me—all the pizza you can eat. And if the whole school reads two thousand books by the end of April—*two thousand books*—I'll . . ."

He paused for emphasis, until the class was completely silent, before he finished his sentence.

"I'll shave off my beard!"

The class whooped and hollered.

"Any questions?"

Kelsey didn't want to be the only one raising

her hand, but she had to ask. "What about the *person* who reads the most books? Does she get a prize, too?"

Simon turned around and stared at her. She stared right back.

"Yes! I'm glad you asked! The person who reads the most books in each class will get his or her name on a permanent plaque in the school library, as well as a special signed certificate to take home. And, of course, you'll help your class win the pizza party. And you'll help me lose my beard."

He laughed again, but the laugh was less big and booming this time.

Maybe he was hoping that Franklin School couldn't read two thousand books in a month. If so, he was wrong. Kelsey could practically read two thousand books all by herself. Mrs. Molina's class had as good as won the pizza party, thanks to Kelsey Green, reading queen.

She could already see her name engraved on the library plaque, for future generations of Franklin School students to behold with admiration.

"Okay?" Mr. Boone asked the class.

"Okay!" they shouted, Kelsey loudest of all.

He hoisted himself off Mrs. Molina's desk, and she quickly moved her stack of papers back into place.

Kelsey closed *The Secret Garden* and tucked it inside her desk. It would be book number one. One down; one thousand, nine hundred ninety-nine to go.

"All right, third graders!" Mr. Boone called to them as he headed out the door. "Ready, set, read!"

2

Kelsey wanted to spend the evening reading *The Secret Garden*. But her mother made her go to her brother's eighth-grade band concert. Kelsey's whole family always went to everything. Her mother called it "being a family."

Usually Kelsey liked listening to Dylan play the trombone and cheering as Sarah scored for the high school girls' varsity basketball team. It would be fun having her whole family in the audience when Mr. Boone shaved off his beard, maybe announcing first that it was because of Kelsey Green that he had to do it.

But right this minute being a family was taking up too much time. Valuable time that could be spent reading.

"Do I have to go?" Kelsey asked.

Her mother didn't bother answering the question. "You can bring your book and read during intermission."

"Can I read during the concert, too? When Dylan's band isn't playing?"

"It'll be too dark to read."

Apparently her mother had forgotten that Kelsey had her own pencil-sized flashlight.

So Kelsey read through the sixth-grade band—terrible!—and the seventh-grade band—better—and closed *The Secret Garden* only when the eighth-grade band took the stage. She knew better than to ask if she could keep on reading up until the minute when Dylan had his solo.

When she went to bed that night, she still had five chapters to go.

*   *   *

The first thing Kelsey saw when she walked into the front doors of Franklin School at eight o'clock the next morning was a huge sheet of paper as wide as an entire classroom. The paper was taped to the wall, stretching from floor to ceiling.

On the paper was an enormous chart, with a column for every class in the school, three classes at every grade level from kindergarten to fifth grade. The columns were waiting to be colored in as students started reading.

Next to the big chart were taped two smaller squares of paper. One had the date on it: April 1. The other had the number of books read so far by everybody in the school: 0.

If only Kelsey had finished *The Secret Garden* last night. She could have had the first book read by anybody in Franklin School.

After the bell rang and the students were all in their seats, Mrs. Molina asked, "Did anyone finish reading a book last night?"

Only one hand went up.

Simon Ellis.

Kelsey hoped that this was an April Fool's Day joke, but it wasn't.

"Excellent, Simon!" Mrs. Molina said. "I'll be sending our class total every morning to Mr. Boone, so I'll let him know that we have one book read already. Class, I'm counting on all of you to follow Simon's example."

If it hadn't been for Dylan's stupid band concert, Mrs. Molina could have been saying, "I'm counting on all of you to follow Simon and *Kelsey*'s example."

Mrs. Molina showed the class a stack of photocopied sheets of paper placed on one corner of her very neat desk. She held up a sample sheet. Printed on it was the shape of a slug, or perhaps a chubby, stubby worm.

"These are our bookworms," Mrs. Molina explained. "When you finish reading a book, take one of these bookworms. On it, write your name and the name of your book, and put it in the bookworm folder I've made for each of you. The folders are in that file box over by the window, on top of our classroom library shelves. You can take blank bookworms home with you, too, to fill out there."

Mrs. Molina beamed as Simon filled out his bookworm and put it in his folder in the worm box.

Kelsey scowled.

She read *The Secret Garden* during silent reading time—not daring to read any more during math—and finished it at lunch. But by the time she had her first bookworm ready to put into the box, three other kids had bookworms as well, and Simon had a second one.

Kelsey noticed that Simon's second book was

very skinny. It didn't have 311 pages like *The Secret Garden.*

She raised her hand. "How long does a book have to be to get a bookworm?"

Mrs. Molina adjusted her glasses, the way she did when she was thinking.

"One hundred pages," she said.

A chorus of groans arose.

"*Sarah, Plain and Tall* only has 58 pages, and it won the Newbery Medal," Annika pointed out.

Mrs. Molina adjusted her glasses again. "The number of pages isn't what matters," she corrected herself. "What matters is if I think the book is an appropriate choice for third graders."

She glanced over at Cody Harmon. Kelsey knew that Cody read books appropriate for a second grader, or even for a first grader, when he read books at all.

"Or appropriate for *your* reading level," Mrs. Molina said.

Kelsey didn't think that was fair. If Cody got worms for reading short, easy books, she should get worms for them, too. It would be wrong if someone won the best reader prize by reading shorter, easier books than everyone else. Not that Cody was in any danger of winning the best reader prize.

But she didn't say anything. She was going to read *Sarah, Plain and Tall* as soon as Annika was done reading it. And every other short but age-appropriate book she could find.

By the end of the weekend, Kelsey had read five books. When the classroom tally was taken on Monday morning, the start of the first full week of the contest, Simon had read seven. No one else had read more than three, so Kelsey was in second place behind Simon. Annika and Izzy had each read two. Cody hadn't read any.

As the class walked to P.E., Kelsey checked

the chart in the front hallway. Mrs. Molina's third-grade class was in second place behind Mr. Thurston's fifth graders.

Kelsey had no intention of letting herself or her class remain in second place. When her mother came to pick her up from school, her backpack was full of short but age-appropriate books from the classroom library. Annika was coming home with her; Izzy was busy running with the Franklin School Fitness Club, training for a 10K race in May.

Kelsey had suggested to Izzy that she could try holding an open book in front of her as she ran. Izzy had said that was the dumbest idea she had ever heard. She had said it in a way that made Kelsey think that Izzy didn't want to hear any more reading-related suggestions.

"How was your day, girls?" Kelsey's mom asked as Kelsey and Annika climbed into the backseat of the car. Because Kelsey's mom was a stay-at-home mom, she was always the one who gave rides to everybody.

"Good," Annika said, just as Kelsey said, "Terrible."

"Terrible?"

"I don't think it's possible," Kelsey said, "that Simon Ellis read seven books in four days."

"Maybe he's a fast reader," her mother offered.

"I'm a fast reader, and I read *five* books. Of course, Simon probably didn't have to go to any band concerts." Kelsey hoped her mother felt guilty. "And Simon's parents probably don't make him go to bed at nine."

"One of his books was skinny," Annika pointed out.

"Yes, but two of the books he read were fat."

Kelsey really didn't think that Simon could have read two fat books in such a short period of time, plus five others.

He was a good reader, but not that good.

He was a good reader, but not a better reader than Kelsey Green.

Kelsey paused. "Two of the books he *said* he read were fat."

After all, who was checking to see if students were actually reading the books for which they were busily collecting bookworms? It would be so easy for someone who already had a reputation as a top reader to exaggerate just a little tiny bit, with his eyes on a library plaque and a classroom pizza party.

"Now, Kelsey," her mother said.

"Are you thinking what I'm thinking?" Annika asked.

Kelsey said, "I'm thinking that somebody might be cheating."

3

Kelsey and Annika called Izzy once they figured she was home from Fitness Club. They told her to meet them at school fifteen minutes early the next morning to make a top-secret cheater-catcher plan.

That morning, the three of them hid behind a long row of bushes bursting with yellow blossoms at the edge of the school property. Kelsey snapped off one little sprig and tucked it into her short, straight brown hair. It made her feel beautiful, like Helen of Troy, from the short but age-appropriate book of Greek mythology she had been reading the night before. Kelsey of Troy.

"Okay," Kelsey said, calling the meeting to order. "How can we catch Simon cheating?"

"What if he isn't cheating?" Izzy asked. Izzy was always fair to everyone, even boys.

"What if he is?" Annika shot back.

"Well, what *if* he is?" Izzy asked. "No one will know, and our class will win anyway."

Kelsey was shocked. "We don't want to win by *cheating*. We want to win by *reading*."

Besides, she wanted to be the one to have her name immortalized on the plaque as the best reader in the whole class, not some boy cheater.

"Anyway, that's what we're going to find out," Kelsey said. Her Kelsey of Troy flower slid down her hair; she stuck it back in place.

"How?" Izzy asked.

"That's what we need to figure out," Kelsey

explained, trying not to sound impatient. She liked Annika and Izzy equally, but sometimes it took longer for Izzy to *get* things.

"We could spy on him," Izzy suggested. "I could look in the window of his house after school and see if he's reading. If anyone sees me, I'll run really fast. I'll be the spy, because I'm good at running."

Kelsey had been wrong to doubt Izzy. Izzy might be overly fair and slow to catch on sometimes, but she was definitely brave.

"All right," Kelsey said. "Idea number one is spying. Any other ideas?"

"We could make it into a math problem," Annika said. "We count up how many pages Simon reads in a day—how many he *says* he reads—and how many free minutes there are in a day, and then divide the pages by the minutes, or the minutes by the pages, and see if it's humanly possible to read that fast."

Kelsey's head was spinning. "Could you do a math problem like that?"

"Sure, I could do it easy-peasy."

"Any other ideas?" Kelsey asked.

"You haven't had any yet," Izzy pointed out.

"Maybe . . . I could read one of the same books as Simon and say something to him about the book, something *wrong* about the book. And see if he notices. Like, if it was *The Secret Garden*, and he had read it, too, I'd say, 'Wasn't it sad when the secret garden burned down?' And if he says, 'Yes, it was sad,' then I'd know he hadn't really read the book. Because the garden doesn't burn down."

"Which plan should we do?" Annika asked.

Kelsey jammed her Kelsey of Troy flower, which kept on slipping, back behind her ear again.

"All three," she said.

*   *   *

Kelsey had two bookworms to put in her worm folder that morning. While she was over by the worm box, she casually pulled out Simon's folder. Anybody could pull out the wrong folder by mistake. Anyway, the box was conveniently far away from Mrs. Molina's desk.

Simon's folder had eight worms in it, from the last five days. But had they been long books or short books? With big print or small print? Pictures or no pictures?

She needed to write down the titles, but she didn't have a piece of paper with her. Maybe she could remember them in her head. *Frindle* was one. *Dear Whiskers* was another.

"*Frindle. Dear Whiskers*," Kelsey repeated under her breath as she went back to her desk. "*Frindle. Dear Whiskers.*"

"Did you have a question, Kelsey?" Mrs. Molina asked.

Kelsey shook her head.

She started a list on the last page in her spiral-bound language arts notebook. *S.B.*, she wrote on the top of the page. That was code for *Simon's Books*. She wrote down the two titles she had memorized. Now she needed to go back to Simon's folder for the other six.

Notebook in hand, she started toward the worm box, but Mrs. Molina stopped her. "Kelsey, your worms aren't going anywhere." Mrs. Molina gave a small smile, as if she had said something clever. "You can visit them after math time."

Kelsey wanted to say that "visiting her worms" was part of math time. Getting the titles of Simon's other six books was going to help Annika do the most important math problem that had ever been done in the history of Franklin School.

Instead, Kelsey had to sit back down and drag out her math book.

Wait. She remembered one more of Simon's titles. Something about a mouse. *The Mouse and the Motorcycle.* She wrote it down on her S.R. page and then opened her own library book, *Amber Brown Is Not a Crayon,* to see if she could read just one or two pages before math time officially began.

The classroom door opened. Mr. Boone bounced in, bearded and beaming.

Mrs. Molina forced a smile. "Yes, Mr. Boone? We're just starting math."

This time Mr. Boone perched himself not on Mrs. Molina's desk but on the desk of the boy closest to the door.

"Good morning, third graders!" he boomed.

"Good morning, Mr. Boone!" everyone shouted.

"I just wanted to say that I'm very impressed by your good start on the reading contest. No, make that your *great* start."

"Did you do the totals for today yet? Are we number one?" a kid in the back of the room called out.

"Right now, you're still number two, behind Mr. Thurston's fifth graders. But"—Mr. Boone dropped his voice to a loud whisper— "I heard their star reader, Lindsay Conant, is going to be gone all next week on a family trip to Disney World. This could be your chance!"

"Thanks for that encouragement," Mrs. Molina said. Her tone said, *And now it's time for you to go.* Mrs. Molina did love math time more than anything.

"Keep reading!" Mr. Boone ruffled his beard and winked at the class as he turned to walk away.

By the end of the day, Kelsey had made two more trips to visit the worm box and had written down all eight of Simon's titles. Actually, all nine. During silent reading time, Simon had finished *Alvin Ho: Allergic to Girls, School, and Other Scary Things.*

"We can get the number of pages for the books on Amazon.com," Annika said as the three girls walked out of school to get a ride to Kelsey's house with Kelsey's mom.

"How do you know that?" Izzy asked.

Annika shrugged. "I know a lot of things."

An hour later, Annika had gathered all her data, using the computer on Kelsey's desk. Kelsey and Izzy sat side by side on Kelsey's bed, watching as Annika turned on her calculator. This was definitely more exciting than doing fractions with Mrs. Molina. Kelsey had never known that there could be a *reason* for doing a math problem.

She imagined it as a word problem:

Simon Ellis says he has read 9 books with a total of 1,413 pages in 5 days.

If Simon reads 5 hours a day, how many pages would he have to read per minute? IS HE OR IS HE NOT CHEATING?

"So?" Kelsey asked, as Annika finished writing the last number on her page of calculations.

"He'd have to read about a page a minute."

"Could he read a page a minute?" Izzy asked.

"Let's time Kelsey. Of course, some pages have a lot more words than others. Kelsey, pick a book that has kind of average pages."

Kelsey picked *Sarah, Plain and Tall*; Annika had given it to her that afternoon.

"Wait until the clock clicks to the next minute to begin," Izzy commanded. "Okay . . . go!"

Kelsey read as fast as she could. She had just finished the page when Izzy called, "Time!"

"Okay," Annika said. "I guess it's possible that Simon can read a page a minute. But it would be hard to read that fast for a whole entire book. Not to mention nine whole entire books."

"So is he cheating?" Kelsey asked.

Annika turned off her calculator. "We still don't know."

4

By the end of the second full week of the contest, Mr. Thurston's class was still ahead. Maybe their star reader had mailed her worms back from Disney World. Kelsey could picture this famous reader reading on the plane, reading in her hotel room, reading in the line for the Space Mountain ride.

Unfortunately, Simon was still ahead, too. Just by three books, but with both Simon and Kelsey reading as fast as humanly possible—if Simon wasn't cheating—this meant that every time Kelsey read another book, Simon read one, too. Plus, one afternoon Kelsey had to go to Dylan's track meet, and another evening she had to go to some awards ceremony for Sarah.

"Why do I have to go to everything?" Kelsey wailed, when she found out about Sarah's banquet.

"Because you're part of this family," her mother replied serenely.

Kelsey thought her mother could come up with some new lines once in a while.

"Sarah can show me her award when she gets home. You'll put it up in the hallway by our bedrooms, like you do with all our awards, and I'll see it every day for the rest of my life."

"Kelsey," her mother said, less serenely this time.

"How can I ever get an award if I have to spend all my time watching other people get awards?"

Kelsey stomped up to her room and slammed

the door. In the time she had spent arguing with her mother, she could have read five more pages of *Mr. Crumb's Secret*.

The girls hadn't spied on Simon yet. Izzy kept being busy with Fitness Club and softball, which unfortunately meant that she had only read three more books for the classroom total.

Even Annika, who had a less good excuse, had only read six.

Kelsey tried mentioning the contest to Annika one day when the two of them were alone at Kelsey's house.

"How is your reading for the contest coming along?" she asked casually, as if she didn't already know Annika's pitiful worm total perfectly well.

"Don't," Annika said.

"Don't what?" Kelsey said, even though she knew.

"I don't ask you how your fractions are

coming along, do I? Reading is your big thing, not mine."

But reading was different from fractions, in Kelsey's opinion. Not everybody liked fractions; in fact, as far as Kelsey knew, nobody liked fractions except for Annika. But everybody should like reading. And there wasn't a fractions contest the way there was a reading contest. Though, to be fair, Kelsey wasn't sure she would have tried hard on fractions even if there had been a fractions contest with a possible pizza party and a beard-shaving at the end of it.

Kelsey was going to have to accept that she could count on Izzy for running and Annika for math, period.

Kelsey hadn't tried to trick Simon yet, either. Just the thought of it made her heart race and her palms sweat. She knew she'd turn bright red and ruin the whole plan by stammering.

But one of these days they'd do their spying.

And one of these days Kelsey would make herself do her tricking.

Just not quite yet.

Instead, Kelsey decided to work on Cody Harmon. Cody's worm folder was the only folder in the class that was completely empty. In two weeks, Cody had not read one single book, not even a first-grade-level book like *Frog and Toad Together*, which Mrs. Molina would probably consider worm-worthy if it were read by Cody.

Monday morning of week three, Kelsey made a point of sitting next to Cody on the round carpet by Mrs. Molina's rocking chair for the after-lunch read-aloud of *Stuart Little*. As Mrs. Molina was waiting for a few straggling students to take their places, Kelsey asked Cody point-blank, "Why aren't you reading any books for the contest?"

Maybe it was too blunt a thing to ask. Kelsey was better at bluntness than she was at trickery.

Cody turned his pale blue eyes on her. Cody's hair was straight and brown, like hers, but it stood up in a funny way on the top of his head. From all her reading, Kelsey knew that this was called a *cowlick*. Why it was called a *cowlick*, she didn't know. Maybe it would take a cow licking it with her huge pink tongue to make it lie down flat.

"Why aren't you reading?" she repeated.

Cody answered with a question of his own: "Why don't you jump in a lake?"

"You're making us lose!"

"All right, class," Mrs. Molina said in her settle-down voice. "Let's see what happens to Stuart in chapter seven."

Kelsey hardly listened to Stuart's race in a toy sailboat across the pond in Central Park. She was so mad at Cody Harmon! It would take him five minutes to read a Frog and Toad book. He could earn a worm for the glory of his class in just five minutes, and he refused to do it. He was a traitor—a Benedict Arnold! Kelsey had read a biography of Benedict Arnold just yesterday, as a matter of fact. Benedict Arnold lived during the Revolutionary War; he was an American general, but he tried to sell West Point to the British. Ever since then, someone who betrayed his country was called a Benedict Arnold. Well, someone who was a traitor to his third-grade class should be called a Cody Harmon.

During math time on Tuesday, Kelsey was reading a collection of Aesop's fables, little stories that each had a moral at the end. She had been so good at not reading during math time for the last two weeks, but it was too close to the end of the contest now to waste math time doing math.

The first story in the book was about a contest between the wind and the sun to see which was the strongest. The test for being strongest was seeing which one could make the man in the story take off his coat first.

The wind tried to blow off the man's coat, but the more the wind howled, the more tightly the man clutched it. Then the sun took its turn, shining down gently on the man, and the man got so warm that he took off his coat simply because he wanted to. The moral of the story was: "Kindness is stronger than force."

Mrs. Molina called on Kelsey for a fractions problem. This time Kelsey didn't wait for Annika to whisper the correct answer. She blurted out any old wrong answer, so that she could finish the thought that was bursting in her brain.

Kindness is stronger than force.

She had a new plan for dealing with Cody Harmon.

* * *

Luckily, their class had their library time on Tuesday afternoons. Instead of hunting for a new stack of short but age-appropriate books, Kelsey found some appropriate-for-Cody books. She took them over to the big beanbag chair where Cody was sprawled, staring off into space.

"I found you some books," Kelsey said.

"I don't want any books," Cody replied.

"I'm going to help you read them. Here. This one's good. *Henry and Mudge and the Forever Sea.*"

Cody squinted at the cover. "What's a forever sea?"

"It's poetic. It means a big, big sea."

"What's so great about the big, big sea?"

"Read it and find out."

No, that sounded bossy, like something the wind would say.

"Let's read it together." Kelsey smiled: a warm, sunny, take-off-your-coat smile.

"Go read your own book," Cody said.

Kelsey tried to make her voice as coaxing as her smile. "Don't you want to have some worms— well, at least one worm—like everybody else?"

Cody looked as if he was thinking it over. He couldn't like being the only kid in the class without a single worm to his name.

"Please?" Kelsey asked.

Cody didn't say anything, but he let Kelsey sit down cross-legged on the floor next to his beanbag. He could have gotten up and stalked away, but all the kids liked to sit on the squishy beanbag chairs, and the other beanbag chairs were already taken.

Kelsey opened the book to the first page and held it out to him.

"*You* read it," he said.

"You can't get a worm if I read it."

"*You* can get a worm."

Not for reading a first-grade baby book.

Kelsey pointed at the opening lines. She tried to make her smile extra encouraging, as sunny as a smile could be.

Cody read the first page slowly. Kelsey had been wrong: it was going to take him a lot more than five minutes to read about the forever sea.

He stumbled over the words *vacation* and *beach*. Kelsey wasn't sure if she should correct him or not.

What would the sun do?

She decided the sun would just sit there and shine.

She shone through the whole book. Cody finished it two minutes before library time ended. Kelsey would have to come back another time to get her own books, but she didn't mind.

Cody Harmon had earned his first bookworm for Mrs. Molina's class. Kelsey filled it out for

him the minute they got back to their class-room; it was easier to do it herself than to try to talk him into doing it. Talking him into reading the book had been enough for one day.

Go, third grade!

5

Kelsey had been sure Cody would come into school the next day with ten new bookworms from all the Henry and Mudge books she had sent home with him.

He didn't.

"Here are some blank worms for you to fill out," she said, standing next to his desk as the rest of the students were taking their seats before morning announcements and the Pledge of Allegiance. "You know, for all the books you read last night."

"I didn't read any."

"You didn't read *any*?"

Cody's face set in that stubborn way Kelsey had already gotten to know.

Sun, sun, Kelsey reminded herself. But the Aesop fable hadn't said what happened the next day, or the day after that. Did the sun just keep on shining down on the man, whether he took off his coat or not? Did it continue shining down on him warmly and pleasantly every single day?

"Okay," Kelsey said. "That's fine. Really, it's fine. It's completely fine! We can read another one together. At lunch."

Though lunch was when Kelsey had planned to finish reading *Ramona the Pest.* She had only one more chapter left. The book was longer than she had wanted, but the print was pretty big. And Ramona was so much fun to read about—on strike from kindergarten after her teacher scolded her for pulling Susan's boing-

boing curls. Would Ramona ever go back to kindergarten again?

"Do you have your Henry and Mudge books with you?" Kelsey asked. "Did you remember to bring them back to school today?"

Cody opened his desk to show her it was filled to the brim with Henry and Mudge books. He hadn't even bothered to take them home.

"But how could you possibly read them if—?" Kelsey felt her voice rising higher in a gust of windy fury.

She didn't know what she would have said if the morning announcements hadn't clicked on in the nick of time. The thought of all those wasted worm possibilities nearly broke her heart.

After the pledge, as soon as Mrs. Molina told the class to get out their math books, Kelsey put *Ramona the Pest* in place on her lap. She was up to such a good part in *Ramona* that she couldn't bear not to read just a few more pages.

Dimly, she heard Mrs. Molina explaining something about fractions. Maybe something about adding them. Maybe something about subtracting them. She vaguely heard Simon asking some show-offy question that had the word *denominator* in it.

As she read on, Ramona's sister, Beezus, called Ramona a kindergarten dropout.

Beezus teased Ramona for misunderstanding the words of "The Star-Spangled Banner."

Ramona burst into tears and threw her crayons all over the floor.

"Kelsey Green!"

The voice was Mrs. Molina's. But it wasn't coming from the front of the room. It was coming from next to Kelsey's desk.

In an instant, Mrs. Molina had snatched *Ramona the Pest* off Kelsey's lap and was brandishing it in the air for the whole class to see. Kelsey could hear Annika's gasp and Izzy's low moan.

"No wonder you're having trouble with fractions!" Mrs. Molina thundered.

Mrs. Molina had no right telling the whole class how badly Kelsey was doing in math. Of course, from the fact that she got every single answer wrong, except when Annika prompted her, they probably already knew.

Mrs. Molina strode back to her desk, carrying Kelsey's book with her. "I am not returning this to you until three o'clock this afternoon."

How was Kelsey going to finish it in time to get another worm for today?

"Furthermore, I'm not going to let you count this book for the reading contest, Kelsey, because you were reading it at an inappropriate time."

How could there be an inappropriate time for *reading*?

"But—" Kelsey started to protest. "I'm already on page 174!"

"You should have thought of that before you started reading during math time. Now look at problem twenty-one on page 186."

With Mrs. Molina's eyes boring down on her, Kelsey knew Annika wouldn't dare whisper the answer. Usually when Kelsey gave a wrong answer, Mrs. Molina just sighed and called on someone else. This time, Mrs. Molina refused to move on until Kelsey actually understood what the answer was supposed to be.

Finally, Kelsey must have managed to say something right, or at least right enough, and math time was over.

At lunchtime, Kelsey half wanted to give up on Cody and find a *very* short but age-appropriate book she could race through instead. To her surprise, Cody came over to where she was sitting with Annika and Izzy. Without a word, he held out *Henry and Mudge and the Careful Cousin*.

Maybe Cody was finally catching bookworm fever, too. Or maybe he felt guilty for leaving all of his Henry and Mudge books at school. Or maybe he felt sorry for Kelsey for getting in trouble in math. Right now Kelsey didn't care.

She and Cody sat on a bench by the swing set and Cody haltingly read aloud to her. To Kelsey's disappointment, he wasn't reading any better than he had the day before. Probably one 48-page book wasn't enough to turn him into an instant reader.

Kelsey had a sudden thought: reading was as hard for Cody as fractions were for her.

"You're doing great," she said to him, even though he wasn't. But she had to give him credit for trying harder at reading than she was at math.

At three o'clock, as Kelsey was shrugging on her backpack to head out the classroom door and get as far away from her teacher as possible, Mrs. Molina called her name again.

"Kelsey! Don't forget your book!"

Mrs. Molina was offering *Ramona the Pest* to her, with a smile! As if all were forgiven!

"I don't want it now," Kelsey said coldly. "If you won't let me get a worm for it, I'm not going to finish reading it."

Maybe Mrs. Molina would relent. How could she let a student abandon a book as good as *Ramona the Pest* when the student had already read to page 174?

But Mrs. Molina just handed her the book and said, "Oh, Kelsey."

She sounded just like Kelsey's mother.

And sure enough, in the car on the way home, when Kelsey told her mother how unfair Mrs Molina had been, her mother said, "Oh, Kelsey," too.

Kelsey finally broke down and read the last

18 pages of *Ramona the Pest* before she went to bed. But if Mrs. Molina thought Kelsey would ever forgive her for denying her a well-earned worm for 192 whole pages, she was sadly mistaken.

6

Simon was now four worms ahead because of *Ramona the Pest*. It was getting harder for Kelsey to find short but age-appropriate books; she had read almost all of the ones in the school library.

"Do you think Junie B. Jones would count as age-appropriate?" Kelsey asked Annika as they searched the library shelves after school on Thursday. Kelsey had asked her mother to pick them up a bit later.

"No. Junie B. Jones is in kindergarten!"

"So is Ramona. And Ramona is age-appropriate." Or would have been.

"Junie B. Jones is a lot shorter than Ramona. I mean, her books are a lot shorter. With tons of pictures."

"Ramona has pictures, too."

Kelsey knew it was a lost cause. She could ask Mrs. Molina just to be sure, but she couldn't bear the thought of the mean little smile the teacher would give when she said no.

Then Kelsey remembered how many pictures there had been in the biography of Benedict Arnold she had read last week. There were lots of short but age-appropriate biographies. It didn't count against biographies that they had tons of pictures. Biographies were supposed to have tons of pictures so that you could see what everybody looked like long ago.

Her mother must be outside waiting by now. So Kelsey quickly chose a biography of Harriet Tubman, who helped slaves escape on the Underground Railroad, and one of Emily Dickinson, the poet. She wondered if a book of poetry would count as age-appropriate. Poems had all that nice white space around them on each page. Even grownups read poetry, and nobody said they were babyish readers. Kelsey grabbed a book of Emily Dickinson poems, just in case.

"What took you so long?" her mother asked as Kelsey and Annika climbed into the backseat of the car; Izzy was at Fitness Club, as usual.

"I couldn't find any good books." By *good*, Kelsey meant *short*. "Do you think a poetry book is age-appropriate?"

"I don't see why not. But you'll need to ask Mrs. Molina."

Kelsey decided just to fill out a poetry worm and assume it was fine unless she heard otherwise. She certainly wasn't going to ask Mrs. Molina.

By the time they reached Kelsey's house, ten minutes later, she had already read half the

Emily Dickinson poems. Some of them were hard to understand, but nobody said you had to understand every single word in a book in order to get a worm for it.

Some of the poems were wonderful.

"Don't go inside yet," Kelsey said to Annika. "Just listen to this poem."

She started reading:

> *"There is no Frigate like a Book*
> *To take us Lands away,*
> *Nor any Coursers like a Page*
> *Of prancing Poetry."*

"I don't get it," Annika interrupted. "What's a frigate? And what are coursers?"

Kelsey wasn't completely sure what those things were, either. But she knew the poem was about how much Emily Dickinson loved books, and how books could take you anywhere. She

loved the words "prancing Poetry." Poetry did prance, like horses. *Coursers* must be horses. Emily's words gave her a wonderful shivery feeling all over.

"I think a frigate is a ship," she said, for starters.

"So why didn't they say *ship*?"

Kelsey gave up. Some people loved poetry. Some people loved math. But both kinds of people could be friends.

The next day, counting both the Emily Dickinson poetry book and the Emily Dickinson biography, Kelsey had two new worms. Simon had only one. So he was back to being just three worms ahead.

Kelsey didn't think she dared count any more poetry books toward her worm total. But how would she ever catch up to Simon? The reading contest would be over in another week!

"I think," Kelsey said to her friends at lunch, "we're going to have to do some spying this weekend."

Izzy's face lit up. "Bring it on!"

Annika looked pleased, too. "Simon Ellis, your days are numbered!" she said with a cackling chuckle.

Kelsey had a small pang at the thought of what would happen to their class worm total if Simon was caught as a cheater reader. But maybe their class was going to lose to Mr. Thurston's anyway, despite all of Simon's possibly bogus worms. And it would be bitter beyond bearing if a cheater's name was on the library plaque instead of hers. It was going to be awful if his name was on the plaque instead of hers, period.

That evening, Kelsey prepared her spy notebook. In *Harriet the Spy*, Harriet had a special notebook where she wrote down all her observations about everything in big capital letters. Kelsey had read *Harriet the Spy* before the reading contest began. It was much too long to be a reading contest book.

Kelsey wrote:

SIMON HAS TWENTY-FOUR WORMS. I HAVE TWENTY-ONE. I WONDER IF SIMON LOVES READING THE WAY EMILY DICKINSON AND I DO OR IF HE JUST LIKES BEING THE BEST AT EVERYTHING. HE IS AS GOOD AT MATH AS ANNIKA. BUT HE ISN'T A FAST RUNNER LIKE IZZY. I HOPE IZZY CAN RUN FAST ENOUGH TOMORROW. I LEARNED FROM HARRIET THE SPY THAT TERRIBLE THINGS CAN HAPPEN IF SPIES GET CAUGHT.

7

Saturday was warm and sunny. A soft breeze stirred the blossoms on the flowering crabapple tree in Kelsey's front yard.

"The perfect weather for spying!" Izzy said as they all set out in the morning from Kelsey's house.

Annika agreed.

Kelsey herself thought that fog and drizzly rain would have been better weather for spying, not to mention dark of night. The three of them should have planned to meet at midnight. They should have tied strings around their big toes and hung the strings out the window, so that the leader—Izzy, probably—could tug on the strings to wake the others.

Didn't her friends ever *read*?

Annika had looked up Simon's address in the school directory and copied it onto a scrap of paper. He lived just a few blocks away, toward the park.

"If we get caught, we can eat the paper," Annika said.

Maybe her friends did read.

"I saw a spy do that on a TV show once," Annika added.

As they approached Simon's street, Kelsey asked, "What exactly are we going to do when we get there?"

"Spy!" Izzy and Annika answered in unison.

Kelsey felt a sudden surge of doubt. The idea that had seemed so good when it was just an idle suggestion seemed more fraught with peril when it was time actually to carry it out. "But—what if his parents are there? What if his bedroom is upstairs? Will Izzy have to climb a tree to look in the window? What if there isn't a tree? What if Simon sees her looking in?"

She could tell that Izzy and Annika thought these were good questions, questions they probably should have asked themselves sooner.

"We need to make a plan," Kelsey said.

Luckily, she had her *Harriet the Spy* notebook with her, and a pencil.

Annika and Izzy sat down next to her in the shade of another flowering crabapple tree, a block away from Simon's street, as Kelsey started writing.

PLAN FOR SPYING ON SIMON

FIRST WE CASE THE JOINT. THIS MEANS WE WALK BY PRETENDING TO BE GOING SOMEWHERE ELSE.

"What do we do after that?" Annika asked, reading over Kelsey's shoulder.

Kelsey picked up her pencil and continued writing.

IF SOMEONE IS IN THE YARD, WE MAKE CONVERSATION AND GATHER INFORMATION. IF NO ONE IS IN THE YARD, WE SEE IF THERE ARE ANY WINDOWS IZZY CAN LOOK IN.

"What if Izzy gets caught?" Izzy asked.

Kelsey wrote,

IZZY BETTER NOT GET CAUGHT.

Then she closed her notebook and tucked her pencil behind her ear.

When they reached Simon's house, right away Kelsey saw two good things: 1) nobody was in the yard; 2) the house had only one story.

She started to write these facts down in her notebook, but Annika stopped her, sounding almost crabby. "We don't have time for that. They could come out any minute. Izzy needs to spy *now*."

Izzy was practically dancing with excitement as Kelsey and Annika hid behind the tall hedge separating Simon's yard from the yard next door.

"What if she does get caught?" Annika asked Kelsey. "Who eats the paper? You or me?"

As if that were their biggest worry!

"We should have worn disguises," Kelsey said. "Masks, at least."

"Masks would make us look stupid."

"It's better to look stupid than to be stupid," Kelsey shot back.

From her vantage point behind the hedge, she could see Izzy slip around the side of Simon's house and look in the first window. Fortunately, it didn't have any closed blinds or curtains to keep Izzy from peering in. Unfortunately, there was also nothing to keep Simon and his family from peering out.

Now Izzy was behind the house, out of sight.

A few minutes went by. Five? Ten?

"She should be back by now," Annika whispered, even though there was nobody else to hear.

"Maybe she's taking notes," Kelsey whispered back.

But Izzy hadn't taken the *Harriet the Spy* notebook.

Kelsey tried to think of another non-horrible possibility. "Maybe she's—"

A large hand clamped down on Kelsey's shoulder.

She screamed.

Another large hand clamped down on Annika's shoulder.

Annika screamed, too.

"What are you kids doing in my yard?" a deep voice bellowed.

Kelsey thought she might faint. Did people ever faint in real life, or only in books?

When the man let go of them, she made herself look at him. He was about as old as her grandfather, tall, bald-headed, with a beard almost as big and bushy as Mr. Boone's.

"Are you the kids who broke my window last week?" the man demanded. "With your baseball?"

"No!" Kelsey said.

"We've never—" Annika stammered. "We've never been here before."

"Then why are you here now? On private property?"

With the man glaring down at them as if he were about to call the police and have them arrested for trespassing, the only thing Kelsey could think of was the truth. The police would probably torture it out of her, anyway.

"We're spying," she confessed.

Annika's face turned another shade paler. So much for the plan of eating the evidence.

"Spying?" The man sounded as if he had never heard of such a thing. Maybe he didn't read, either.

"On Simon," Kelsey continued faintly. "Simon Ellis. He's in our class at school. Our friend Izzy—"

She turned her head slightly and could see Izzy racing across Simon's lawn, too late to be warned that the real danger lay on the other side of the hedge.

"Izzy was looking in Simon's window to see—"

"To see what?"

"No one was there!" Izzy burst out as she tore around the hedge. "I couldn't find anything!"

She saw the man and stopped, apparently unsure whether to run or to stay with her captured friends.

"To see what?" the man repeated. "Don't you know that there are laws against looking in people's windows?"

Kelsey might as well tell him. "To see if Simon is really reading all the books he says he's reading for the reading contest. At Franklin School. I'm a superfast reader, and I read and read and read, but no matter how many books I read, Simon reads even more. Or he says he does. So we were just checking."

"Checking?"

"To see if he is really reading them or not," Kelsey finished. "Show him the paper," she told Annika.

Maybe there were benefits to not eating the evidence.

"See? We wrote down his address and

everything. We were going to eat the paper if we got caught. But we didn't have time to eat it."

Kelsey waited to see if the man would call the police now.

Instead, he started laughing.

"You kids take the cake!" He laughed again. "Here's some free advice. No more spying! You know what they do to spies when they catch 'em? The firing squad!" But there was a twinkle in his eyes. "And don't play baseball around here, either."

"We won't," Kelsey, Annika, and Izzy promised together.

As they turned to run home, a car pulled into Simon's driveway.

Simon got out of the car. He was carrying a big stack of library books.

Kelsey could practically see Simon's worm folder bulging before her very eyes. Of course, anybody could check out library books. Checking out library books wasn't the same thing as reading library books. But she had to admit that so far the spying part of the top-secret cheater-catcher plan was a failure.

8

Monday morning, Kelsey hurried into school with Annika to check the huge chart in the front hallway, now colored brightly with a different shade of marker for every class.

Franklin School had read a total of 1,752 books. There were just four days left before the reading contest ended on Friday.

"Mr. Boone is going to have to shave his beard!" Annika chortled to Kelsey.

"We haven't read two thousand books yet," Kelsey pointed out.

"We will. Do you want me to prove it to you?"

"Prove it how?"

"With math, duh!"

Annika pulled out her math notebook and scribbled some numbers on a blank page.

"We only need 248 more books. Over the last three weeks, we've averaged 584 books a week."

Kelsey still didn't understand.

"1,752 divided by 3 is 584," Annika explained. "So we only need to read about half that many this week, and we'll win. Kelsey, don't you pay attention in math at all?"

Well, no, Kelsey didn't. Though these days she wasn't reading during math, either.

Mrs. Molina's class, colored with forest-green marker, was only six books behind Mr. Thurston's class, colored with midnight-blue marker, and way ahead of the next closest class.

Mr. Boone popped out of the office to check the chart.

"Start sharpening your razor," Annika told him. Annika wasn't usually as brave as Izzy, but this time she had math to back her up. Plus, you could say anything to Mr. Boone, and he'd just laugh.

He laughed this time, too, but Kelsey thought his laugh had a hollow ring to it. He clutched his beard in a dramatic gesture, to make the girls giggle. But Kelsey didn't think he was pretending.

She couldn't imagine Mr. Boone without his beard. It would be like imagining Izzy without running, or Annika without math, or Kelsey without reading. Instead of looking like a pirate, he'd look like . . . like a round, shiny moon. Mr. Boone would be Mr. Moon.

Kelsey decided to find out once and for all if she could count Junie B. Jones books toward her worm total. The class was gathering for read-aloud time and starting a new book: *When You Reach Me.*

"Why don't you ask Mrs. Molina if we can count Junie B. Jones books?" Kelsey asked Izzy, since Annika had already said that she thought the answer would clearly be no.

"Why don't *you* ask her?"

"She'll say no if I ask, but she might say yes if you do it. Izzy, if I can count Junies, I can beat Simon. I can read a Junie B. Jones book in twenty minutes."

Izzy rolled her eyes. "Don't you ever think about anything except beating Simon?"

"Well, what about you?" Kelsey fired back. "You love winning races, don't you?"

"Yes, but those kinds of races are over in a few minutes. Even marathons are over in a few hours. This dumb reading race has been going on for almost a whole month!"

"It will be over on Friday," Kelsey reminded her.

"Yay for that."

Izzy did raise her hand before Mrs. Molina began reading. "Can we count Junie B. Jones books? For worms?"

Mrs. Molina looked surprised at the question, perhaps because Izzy had only eight worms, and so obviously wasn't devoting great energy to the contest. She adjusted her glasses.

"Well, those books do have a wonderful voice," she said. "And they're very funny."

Kelsey hadn't thought Mrs. Molina would think that *funny* was a good thing.

"But I don't know if Junie is challenging enough for our strongest readers." Mrs. Molina's gaze fell on Kelsey, as if she had just figured out why Izzy was suddenly so interested in boosting her worm total. "I'd rather not make a general rule here, Izzy. As I told all of you before, I want each student to be reading at his or her own level."

So the answer was no, then. No for Kelsey, the strongest reader in the class.

Or at least the second-strongest.

"No!" Kelsey said at dinner Tuesday night. "I am not going to another band concert! Dylan just had a band concert!"

"That was concert band." Dylan speared a meatball and waved it in the air as he continued talking. "This is jazz band. It's different."

"You're still playing trombone, aren't you? Trombone, trombone, trombone!"

Dylan swallowed his meatball. "*I* don't care if you don't come."

"*I* care," Kelsey's mother said. "Kelsey, I know you're obsessed with the reading contest these days. But you're still part of this—"

Kelsey cut her off. "I hate this family!"

She jumped up from the table so suddenly that her glass of milk went flying. Fine! The

rest of them could clean it up together, as a family activity.

"Oh, let her stay home," she heard Sarah say as she fled up the stairs to her room. Well, maybe Kelsey didn't hate Sarah. Or Dylan.

"She's only eight! She can't stay home all by herself." That was her mother's voice.

". . . just this once?" That was her father's voice. Maybe she didn't hate her father, either.

Up in her room, Kelsey threw herself crying on her bed. She was too angry even to read the last few pages of *The Mouse of Amherst*, about a mouse who lived in Emily Dickinson's house and helped her write her poetry.

There was a knock, and her mother pushed the door open. Kelsey buried her face deeper into her pillow.

"Kelsey, look at me."

Kelsey made herself look. Her mother wasn't smiling, but she didn't look furious, either.

"Kelsey, you are going to go back downstairs and apologize to everyone for what you said. You are going to wipe up the milk you spilled. And then, just this once, we'll drop you off at the public library so that you can do your reading while the rest of us are at your brother's concert."

Kelsey leaped off the bed and hugged her mother. She didn't hate any of them anymore.

"I don't really hate this family," she whispered, with her face against her mother's shoulder.

"I know," her mother said, stroking Kelsey's hair.

"But the reading contest ends on Friday!"

Kelsey couldn't hear what her mother said next, but it sounded like "Hooray."

* * *

It was strange being in the library alone in the evening, without Annika or Izzy, without Dylan or Sarah or her parents. Kelsey sat down in one of the large, comfy chairs in the children's room, next to the window, across from the fireplace that on this spring evening had no fire burning.

She tried not to think how she could have been sitting next to Sarah in the middle-school auditorium, poking her whenever a sixth-grade clarinet squealed or a sixth-grade trumpet squawked. She tried not to think of how her father would reach over and take her mother's hand when Dylan stood up to play. It was worth it to have two whole hours all to herself, with nothing to do but read.

She opened *The Mouse of Amherst*. Emily Dickinson had been a recluse. Kelsey knew from her reading that a recluse is someone who never comes out of her house. Emily Dickinson stayed inside her house for twenty years, writing poetry. If only Kelsey could be a reading recluse, at least until Friday.

In the chair across from Kelsey sat the only other kid who was in the library that evening, a tall girl, somewhat overweight, wearing glasses. Maybe a fifth grader.

Kelsey looked at her again. Her heart skipped a beat.

She recognized that girl. It was Lindsay Conant. The famous fifth-grade reader! Kelsey felt a surge of kinship for this girl who also loved reading enough to come alone to the library on a Tuesday evening.

"What are you reading?" Kelsey asked.

Lindsay didn't look up from her book, so Kelsey asked again, louder this time. "What are you reading?"

Lindsay startled, visibly annoyed. She didn't bother answering Kelsey's question directly, but held up her book so that Kelsey could catch a glimpse of the cover: *A Little Princess*. *A Little Princess* was by the same author as *The Secret Garden*. Kelsey had been dying to read it, but it was too long a book to read until after the contest was over.

"Is it wonderful?" Kelsey whispered.

Lindsay snapped the book shut and stalked over to a different chair on the far side of the room. Then she resumed reading.

Okay, be that way!

Kelsey forced herself to start reading, too, but it was hard to keep her thoughts on her book.

Of course the famous fifth-grade reader would want to be left undisturbed. That was why they both had come to the library, after all: not to talk about reading, but to read. Still, Kelsey's heart stung at the older girl's rude crabbiness.

Then Kelsey had a guilty thought: was she herself, the soon-to-be-famous third-grade reader, turning as crabby and rude as the famous fifth-grade reader?

9

By Wednesday morning, the Franklin School total stood at 1,915 books.

"See?" Annika said to Kelsey, as they hurried in before the first bell to look at the huge wall chart.

Kelsey didn't see.

"We only have eighty-five books to go," Annika explained. "For two whole days and fifteen classes of kids, not counting kinder-gartners, who can't really read: five grades, three classes per grade. So each class only has to read five more books—well, five and a half books—and we'll be there."

"You can't get a worm for reading half a book."

"Oh, Kelsey," Annika said.

Mr. Thurston's class was now just two books ahead. Simon was just two books ahead of Kelsey, too.

During math, Kelsey gazed down at her empty lap, where a tempting book should have been. Instead, she used math time to plan out which books she was going to read next. Mrs. Molina hadn't rejected her poetry bookworms, so apparently it *was* all right to read poetry books. Kelsey had four more poetry books picked out. And she had found a biography of Amelia Earhart that was half pictures. She wondered if she had to read every word of every caption, or just the text.

"Kelsey," Mrs. Molina called in her gleeful "gotcha" voice.

But before Mrs. Molina could ask her some hideous math question that she wouldn't be able to answer, the classroom door opened and in bounded Mr. Boone.

Mr. Boone plunked himself down on Mrs. Molina's desk, perilously close to her glass vase of artificial flowers. Mrs. Molina steadied it before it could go flying and carried it carefully to a safe position on the top of her filing cabinet.

"Good morning, third graders!" Mr. Boone shouted.

"Good morning, Mr. Boone!" they shouted back.

"I know some of you think that Franklin School is going to get to two thousand books by Friday."

The class cheered.

"Personally, I don't."

The class booed—good-natured, happy boos.

"I know I told you that if you read two thousand books, I'd shave my beard. I've been thinking about this, and I've decided that isn't a big enough forfeit. Anybody can shave a beard."

But not everybody had a beard as big and bushy as Mr. Boone's, a beard it had probably taken him ten years to grow.

Some murmurs came from the back of the room, but no one said anything. Despite his jovial grin, Mr. Boone didn't seem to be in the mood for laughing.

"I've decided"—Mr. Boone paused for emphasis—"that if Franklin School reads two thousand books by Friday—and I don't think you possibly can—then I'll"—he paused again, longer this time—"I'll kiss a pig!"

Some of the kids cheered, but Kelsey could tell they did it only because Mr. Boone clearly expected them to. These were halfhearted, disappointed cheers.

"So I need your help," Mr. Boone said. He beamed a hopeful smile at the class.

"I need your help," he went on, "finding a pig. The right kind of *kissable* pig!"

He laughed his famous booming laugh, answered by a few faint, scattered giggles.

Kelsey looked around the room. Nobody at Franklin School was going to have a pig, or know anybody who did. The only pigs Kelsey knew were Wilbur from *Charlotte's Web* and Lester from *Mrs. Piggle-Wiggle's Magic*. If Mr. Boone didn't find a pig, he'd have to shave his beard, after all.

"No one?" Mr. Boone said sadly, after a long moment of silence with no hands raised.

Then, from the back of the room, came one low, shy voice.

"I have a pig," Cody Harmon said.

"I didn't know you had a pig," Kelsey said to Cody as they sat down on the playground at lunch to read *Henry and Mudge and the Best*

Day of All. Cynthia Rylant had certainly written a lot of Henry and Mudge books. A school could practically get to two thousand worms by reading nothing but Henry and Mudge books.

"You never asked me if I did," Cody replied.

That was true. Kelsey didn't know anything about Cody Harmon except that he was a slow reader and had a cowlick. She had been too busy accumulating worms to make idle chit-chat.

"Do you want to meet my pig?" Cody asked. "Before I bring him in to school on Friday?"

Meeting Cody's pig meant going to Cody's house after school. It could mean going to Cody's house with a huge stack of Henry and Mudge books. It could mean that Mrs. Molina's class would beat Mr. Thurston's class in the Franklin School reading contest.

"Yes!" Kelsey said. "I'd love to!"

When Kelsey's mother arrived at school to pick the girls up for their ride home, Kelsey had Cody with her, and the world's heaviest backpack filled with fifteen new Henry and Mudge books. Luckily, the Franklin School library seemed to have a full set.

"Can I go to Cody's house?" Kelsey begged as she climbed into the front seat next to her mother. "To read—I mean, to meet Cody's pig? Cody has a pig, and now Mr. Boone is going to kiss it if we read two thousand books by Friday. Oh, and this is Cody."

Her mother looked startled, but said, "I don't see why not." She gave Cody a friendly smile, and he grinned in return.

"Can you drive us there? Cody takes the bus, and I'm not signed up to be a bus rider. And Annika and Izzy want to meet the pig, too, but then can you drive them home so I can stay a little longer, and then come to get me afterward?"

Kelsey didn't look over at Cody as she said it. She hoped Cody would let her stay longer than the others so they could get some reading done. To her relief, he didn't say that she couldn't.

"Of course," her mother said.

Kelsey leaned over and gave her mother a big hug. She was willing to go to ten band concerts now.

Before Cody got on the bus, he gave Kelsey's mom directions to his house, on the outskirts of town. He seemed more confident now that he was the Franklin School pig-owning celebrity.

Kelsey's car arrived at Cody's place a few minutes before the bus. Kelsey saw that Cody lived on an actual farm, complete with a barn and even a silo. Cody could be young Almanzo Wilder from *Farmer Boy*.

While Kelsey's mother chatted with Cody's mother, Cody took Kelsey, Annika, and Izzy to the pigpen to meet his pig.

"But I'm going to stay even after I meet him," Kelsey reminded Cody. "So we can read," she added.

Cody's pig was enormous. *Some pig*, indeed! He was also hairy and dirty.

"I'll wash him before I bring him in to school," Cody said.

Kelsey tried to imagine the pig—Cody said his name was Mr. Piggins—in a bathtub filled with soapy bubbles, being scrubbed with a washcloth.

"I wash him with a hose," Cody said. "I could wash him now, to show you how I do it."

"Maybe after we finish reading," Kelsey said. Though she was planning on reading for a long, long time, if she could coax Cody into doing it.

The others drove away. Cody's mother brought out glasses of milk and cookies. Her hair was straight and brown like Cody's, but she didn't have a cowlick. Maybe only boys had cowlicks.

"Where do you want to read?" Kelsey asked Cody.

Cody shrugged.

"Let's read to Mr. Piggins," Kelsey said.

So Kelsey and Cody sat under the shade of the newly leafed tree on the grass by Mr. Piggins's pen.

Cody read *Henry and Mudge in Puddle Trouble*.

He read *Henry and Mudge Get the Cold Shivers*.

He read *Henry and Mudge and the Bedtime Thumps*.

By the time he had read *Henry and Mudge and the Long Weekend*, plus seven other books in between, Kelsey said, "You know what, Cody? You read ten times better than you did two weeks ago."

He really did.

Cody gave a lopsided grin.

"I think," Kelsey said, "that you are ready to read chapter books. Like the Junie B. Jones or the Magic Tree House books."

Mr. Piggins gave a grunt, as if in approval.

"But we aren't going to start reading chapter books until next week," Kelsey said. "After the contest."

"We still have to read books after the contest?" Cody asked, sounding alarmed.

Kelsey stared at him. "Don't you like Henry and Mudge?" she finally asked.

"Sure," Cody said. "They're all right."

Pigs, Kelsey noted to herself. After the contest ended, she was going to see if she could find Cody some chapter books about pigs.

10

Did you really read all those books?" Mrs. Molina demanded when Cody presented her with eleven new worms on Thursday morning. "In one night?"

Kelsey answered for him. "Uh-huh, he did. He read them to me. To me and Mr. Piggins. His pig."

Cody had filled out all his own bookworms for them, too.

Mrs. Molina still looked skeptical, so Kelsey went on. "You should hear him read now, Mrs. Molina. Ask him to read you a Henry and Mudge book."

Then she wondered if that had been the right thing to say. She wanted Mrs. Molina to believe that Cody now read well enough to have read eleven Henry and Mudge books in one night, but not so well that he shouldn't be getting worms just for reading Henry and Mudge books.

Mrs. Molina sighed. "I believe you, Kelsey."

Then Mrs. Molina turned to Cody. "I'm certainly impressed at how hard you've been working, Cody. Do you realize that you now have the third highest bookworm total for our entire class?"

Cody beamed.

Kelsey beamed, too.

When the class worm totals were added up and posted on the chart outside the office, Mrs. Molina's class was seven books ahead of Mr. Thurston's. Kelsey knew that Cody and Mr. Piggins deserved most of the credit.

Simon was still two books ahead of Kelsey.

Helping Cody read to Mr. Piggins had used up hours of Kelsey's own reading time, but it had been worth it to see Cody's smile at Mrs. Molina's praise. But she would still be heartbroken if Simon won and she didn't. She wouldn't be able to bear it if Simon won!

So today was the day Kelsey had to carry out part three of the top-secret cheater-catcher plan. Today was the day she had to trick Simon into admitting that he was cheating.

If he was cheating.

Kelsey hoped that he was, so that she could be the class reading champion.

She hoped that he wasn't, so that Mrs. Molina's class could beat out the entire school.

Either way, today was the day she had to find out.

Kelsey flipped through Simon's worm folder as the others were lining up to go to P.E.

"Kelsey, your worms aren't going anywhere,"

Mrs. Molina said, with her usual attempt at wit. Obviously, she didn't realize that Kelsey was checking Simon's worms, not her own.

"Goodbye, worms! Be good!" Kelsey said loudly, to show Mrs. Molina that she wasn't the only one who could make supposedly amusing comments about Kelsey's love for her worms. She had seen what she needed to see. She and Simon had read at least three of the same books: *Sarah, Plain and Tall*, a biography of Eleanor Roosevelt, and—she couldn't believe it—*The Secret Garden*.

The Secret Garden didn't seem like the kind of book a boy would like. It wasn't *The Dead Body in the Secret Garden*, or *The Ghost in the Secret Garden*. Though Colin's dead mother was sort of like a ghost. And she did die in the garden, so that was sort of like a dead body—in fact, it *was* a dead body. But it wasn't the main part of the story.

At lunch, Kelsey didn't read any more books

with Cody, now that Cody had more worms than most of the kids in the class, plus was so good at reading on his own. She left Annika and Izzy behind and went over to where Simon was sitting all by himself on a bench at the edge of the playground. Reading, of course.

She didn't feel brave enough, or tricky enough, to say something completely false about the book, the way she had planned before. She was going to try a more direct, but still tricky, approach.

"You read *The Secret Garden*, didn't you?" she blurted out.

She was afraid he'd snap his book shut and stomp away, like the famous fifth-grade reader, but he didn't. He closed his book, keeping his finger in his place.

"Have *you* read it?" he asked.

"Uh-huh." Kelsey tried to think of what to say next.

"What was your favorite part?" Simon asked.

Was *he* trying to trick *her*? "What was *your* favorite part?" she shot back.

"I liked when Mary heard someone crying in the night," Simon said. "And then it turned out to be Colin."

"I liked when Colin was having one of his tantrums, and Mary had a tantrum, too, and told him that there was nothing wrong with him but temper and hysterics," Kelsey said.

"But the best part," Simon said, "was just—"

"The garden." Kelsey finished his sentence.

"The garden," Simon repeated. "How it came to life. With all the flowers that were growing in it. And how it sort of brought Mary and Colin back to life, too." He hesitated. "Do you think that's dumb?"

"What's dumb?"

"Liking the garden?"

"No!" Kelsey said. "Nobody could really read the book and not love the garden."

Simon glanced down at his book, where his finger still marked his page.

"You can go back to reading," Kelsey said. "I need to read, too."

Kelsey found Annika waiting for her by the edge of the playground. Izzy had joined a pickup softball game.

"So?" Annika asked. "Is Simon cheating?"

"No," Kelsey said. "He isn't."

11

Kelsey read through dinner. Nobody tried to stop her. She read past her bedtime.

"The contest does end tomorrow," she heard her mother say to her father. Her mother! Taking her side!

Kelsey couldn't hear what her father said next, but she thought it might have been "About time."

When Kelsey arrived at school on Friday morning to present her final worm total for the contest deadline, she had read a total of thirty-seven books in the month of April.

"How many do you have?" she asked Simon, who was pulling completed bookworms out of his backpack in the coat cubby.

"How many do *you* have?" he asked.

"I asked first."

Simon still paused. Then he said, "Thirty-seven."

"Me, too!"

Kelsey hadn't beaten Simon, but at least they had tied. She felt better about not beating him now that she knew that he had loved *The Secret Garden* the same way she did. It seemed right that two people who loved the same book in the same way should have the same worm total.

"They can put both of our names on the plaque," she said, beaming.

Simon returned her grin.

"Where's Mr. Piggins?" Kelsey turned to ask Cody, who had come into the cubby right behind her, pigless, not that Kelsey had expected that Mr. Piggins would spend the day in their class, math time and all.

"My dad is bringing him in his pickup this afternoon, right before the assembly."

"Do you think Mr. Boone is going to try to back out of kissing Mr. Piggins the way he backed out of shaving his beard?" Kelsey asked.

"I think *Mr. Piggins* is going to try to back out of kissing *him*," Cody said.

Annika and Izzy had come into the coat cubby, too.

"Do you think it's fair that Mr. Boone backed out of shaving off his beard?" Izzy asked. "Changing the rules in the middle of the contest?"

"No," Annika said. "I mean, what if he said that instead of a pizza party there was going to be a . . . a spinach-eating party?"

"But . . ." Kelsey wasn't sure how she was going to finish her sentence. "Mr. Boone loves his beard so much."

"I still think he should shave it," Izzy said. "He *said* he would."

"I think so, too," Annika said.

Then Simon chimed in. "Me, too."

"Me, too," Cody said, "except that I'm glad that he's going to kiss Mr. Piggins."

Kelsey didn't know what to think.

During morning announcements, Mr. Boone didn't reveal which class had read the most. He said the final scores were still being tallied, and the winning class would be announced at the assembly.

"But it's looking as if I may have to kiss that pig, after all!" Mr. Boone finished.

Kelsey could picture him as he said it, happily stroking the beard that wasn't going to have to be shaved off.

Then and there Kelsey decided that the others were right. Mr. Boone should have to kiss a pig *and* shave his beard.

He really should.

The whole school crowded into the gym for the assembly, four hundred students sitting criss-cross applesauce on the scuffed wooden floor. Kelsey could see Mr. Piggins waiting outside the gym door in the school parking lot with Cody's father, who also had a cowlick.

Mr. Boone bounced over to the microphone, beaming with delight.

He announced the grand total for Franklin School: 2,147 books!

He announced the winning class: Mrs. Molina's third grade!

Then he began to read the names of the top readers in each room. The winners from each class in the lower grades filed up to get their certificates. Then came the winners from the other third-grade classes.

Then: "Simon Ellis and Kelsey Green!"

Kelsey heard Annika and Izzy's cheers as she came up on the stage in the front of the gym, clutching a plastic bag behind her back.

As Mr. Boone handed Simon and Kelsey their certificates, Kelsey stood on tiptoe to reach the microphone.

"Mr. Boone?" She made herself go on. "Our class is the winning class, and a bunch of us think you should still have to shave your beard. Because you said you would."

Simon helped her. "And kiss Mr. Piggins, too. But you can't change your mind about shaving your beard."

Kelsey handed him the cordless electric razor that her mother had brought in to give her right before the assembly. Kelsey had called her from the school phone at lunchtime, whispering into the receiver so that the school secretary wouldn't hear.

Mr. Boone glowered down at them. For the first time ever in Kelsey's years at Franklin School, the principal actually looked angry.

The whole school was chanting now, "Beard! Beard! Beard!"

Then Mr. Boone started to laugh. He laughed until tears ran down his face and trickled into his beard. Relieved, Kelsey laughed with him.

"All right, Miss Kelsey and Mr. Simon." Mr. Boone gave one last gasping chuckle. "It was wrong of me to break our agreement, I admit it. I just—well, I'm so used to my beard. I hadn't quite realized how extraordinarily fond I am of it. But because of Franklin School's astonishing accomplishments this month, I will kiss your pig. And then I'll keep my promise and—goodbye, beard!"

The gymnasium roared.

The fourth- and fifth-grade winners hurried up to get their certificates.

Cody's father led Mr. Piggins onto the stage, to thunderous applause. The pig balked a bit as they approached the center of the stage, but Cody's father leaned down and said something soothing into his ear, and Mr. Piggins continued over to where Mr. Boone was standing.

Mr. Boone stooped down and planted an awkward kiss on the top of Mr. Piggins's head, sort of a practice kiss. Then he gave a very quick, darting peck on the pig's hairy snout. It definitely wasn't a long, romantic kiss, like in the movies, but it did count as a kiss. Mr. Piggins didn't seem to mind. He just stood there, probably puzzled as to why an entire gymnasium full of kids was cheering.

And then the music teacher led the students in singing patriotic songs, while Mr. Boone disappeared from the stage for a few minutes.

They sang "My Country, 'Tis of Thee."

They sang "America the Beautiful."

They sang "You're a Grand Old Flag."

When the song came to an end, the music teacher played a few fanfare chords on the upright piano by the stage.

Mr. Boone reappeared through the side door of the gymnasium: their new beardless principal.

His beard was gone, every single whisker. He could have been an ordinary principal at somebody else's school, not the pirate principal of the best reading school in the world.

But then he laughed. Nobody else laughed like that man. When he laughed, he was still Mr. Boone.

Before dinner that night, Kelsey showed her family her certificate; her mother had been at the assembly to see her get it, but her father had

been at work, and Sarah and Dylan had been at school.

"They're going to put our names on the plaque, Simon's and mine and all the other winners', this weekend. And the plaque is going to be hanging up in the library on Monday, Mr. Boone said. And he said that by Monday he's going to start growing back his beard."

"So what do you want to do tonight to celebrate?" her father asked. "It's your night, Kelsey. The sky's the limit! Do you want to go out for dinner? Go to a movie? Or I think there's a concert in the park."

Kelsey shook her head. She knew exactly what she wanted to do to celebrate.

She had *A Little Princess* already checked out from the school library.

"What do I want to do?"

She smiled at all of them.

"Read!"